Alien Tale

First published in this edition 2015

British Library Cataloguing in Publication Data (CIP) is available for this title.

Printed in Malta by Melita Press.

ISBN 978 1 78322 135 6

Visit our website: www.readzonebooks.com

Alien Tale

Christine Moorcroft
and Cinzia Battistel

Two aliens look at the Earth from space.

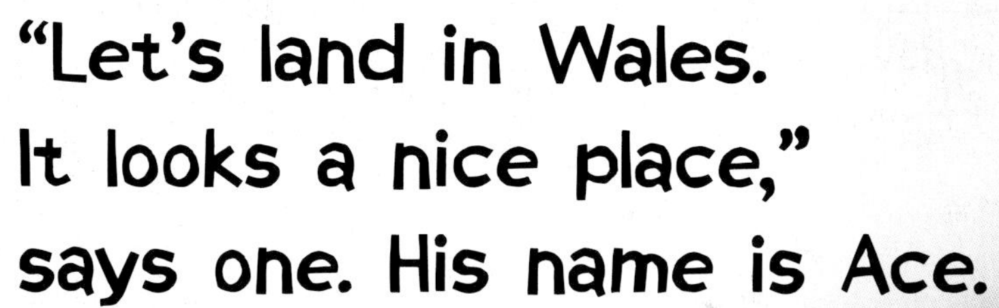
"Let's land in Wales.
It looks a nice place,"
says one. His name is Ace.

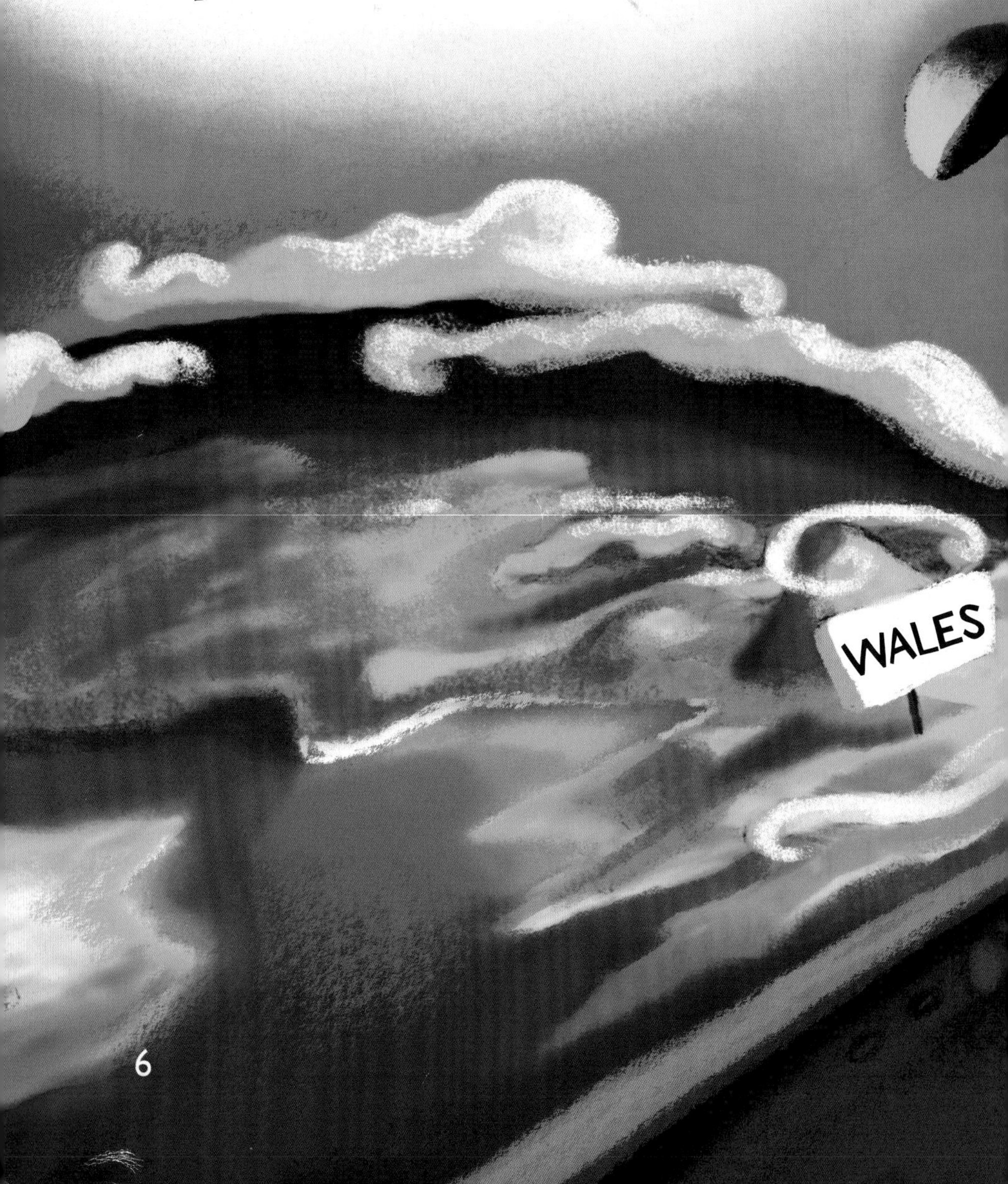

“After breakfast,” says another. Her name is May.

She always has a lot to say.

They stop and look at lots of angels...

...as they munch their
toasted bagels.

But as they feast on
eggs and bacon...

...they forget how long the meal has taken.

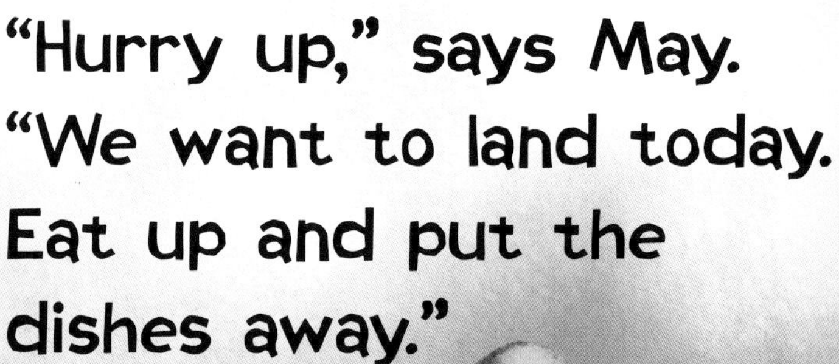

"Hurry up," says May.
"We want to land today.
Eat up and put the
dishes away."

They go over the hills,
and across a plain,

and steer the spaceship
down a lane.

Then, "Wait!" says May.
"This isn't Wales...
it's Spain! Let's stay
and have a lazy holiday."

Then a lady wearing grey
calls, "Hola! No, no way.
No spaceships here...
it's a motorway!
Stop over there for your holiday."

PLAYA

"This place is great,"
call Ace and May.
"Come on, let's play!"

Did you enjoy this book?

Look out for more *Redstart* titles – first rhyming stories for beginning readers

Alien Tale by Christine Moorcroft and Cinzia Battistel
ISBN 978 1 78322 135 6

A Mouse in the House by Vivian French and Tim Archbold
ISBN 978 1 78322 416 6

Batty Betty's Spells by Hilary Robinson and Belinda Worsley
ISBN 978 1 78322 136 3

Croc by the Rock by Hilary Robinson and Mike Gordon
ISBN 978 1 78322 143 1

Now, Now, Brown Cow! by Christine Moorcroft and Tim Archbold
ISBN 978 1 78322 132 5

Old Joe Rowan by Christine Moorcroft and Elisabeth Eudes-Pascal
ISBN 978 1 78322 138 7

Pear Under the Stairs by Christine Moorcroft and Lisa Williams
ISBN 978 1 78322 137 0

Pie in the Sky by Christine Moorcroft and Fabiano Fiorin
ISBN 978 1 78322 134 9

Pig in Love by Vivian French and Tim Archbold
ISBN 978 1 78322 142 4

Tall Story by Christine Moorcroft and Neil Boyce
ISBN 978 1 78322 141 7

The Cat in the Coat by Vivian French and Alison Bartlett
ISBN 978 1 78322 140 0

Tuva by Mick Gowar and Tone Eriksen
ISBN 978 1 78322 139 4